# MYTHS AND HEROES

 publications international, ltd.

WELCOME TO YOUR MYTHS & HEROES ALL-INCLUSIVE TOUR! I'M PAN, AND I'LL BE YOUR GUIDE ON THIS FANTASTICAL JOURNEY. OUR FIRST STOP IS FABULOUS MOUNT OLYMPUS, HOME OF THE GREEK GODS! BEFORE WE MOVE ON TO OUR NEXT SITE, SEE IF YOU CAN CATCH A GLIMPSE OF THESE FAMOUS FOLKS AS THEY WORK AND PLAY.

HEPHAESTUS

ZEUS

DIONYSUS

ARTEMIS

APHRODITE

ATHENA

POSEIDON

NOT EVERY MYTHOLOGICAL FIGURE LIVES ON MOUNT OLYMPUS. INTERESTING CREATURES AND SPECIAL HUMANS CAN BE FOUND ALL OVER THE PLACE. IT LOOKS LIKE SOME OF THEM HAVE GOTTEN TOGETHER FOR A LITTLE SHINDIG TODAY. LET'S STOP BY FOR SOME HORS D'OEUVRES AND SAY HELLO TO SOME OF THE FAMOUS GUESTS.

PYGMALION

NARCISSUS

PROMETHEUS

KING MIDAS

ATLAS

PEGASUS

ARACHNE

JASON

THE GRACES

MEET HERACLES, ONE OF THE MOST FAMOUS—AND HANDSOME—HEROES YOU'LL FIND THIS SIDE OF THE ACROPOLIS. HE'S ALWAYS PERFORMING ONE IMPOSSIBLE FEAT OR ANOTHER. AFTER YOU HIT THE CONCESSION STANDS, SEARCH THIS PARADE BEING THROWN IN HIS HONOR FOR SOME OF THESE ITEMS FEATURING THE GREAT HERO.

SOFT DRINK

MAGAZINE

BANNER

T-SHIRT

STREET SIGN

SHOE

BILLBOARD

NOW WE'RE OFF TO THE ISLAND OF CRETE, WHERE WE'LL CATCH UP WITH ANOTHER GREAT HERO, THESEUS. WHEN HE HEARD THAT A GREAT HALF-MAN, HALF-BULL BEAST CALLED THE MINOTAUR WAS CAUSING TROUBLE, THESEUS KNEW HE HAD TO OFFER HIS HELP. HE'S ABOUT TO ENTER A GREAT LABYRINTH TO SEARCH FOR THE BEAST. CAN YOU HELP HIM FIND HIS WAY THROUGH THE MAZE TO SLAY THE MINOTAUR?

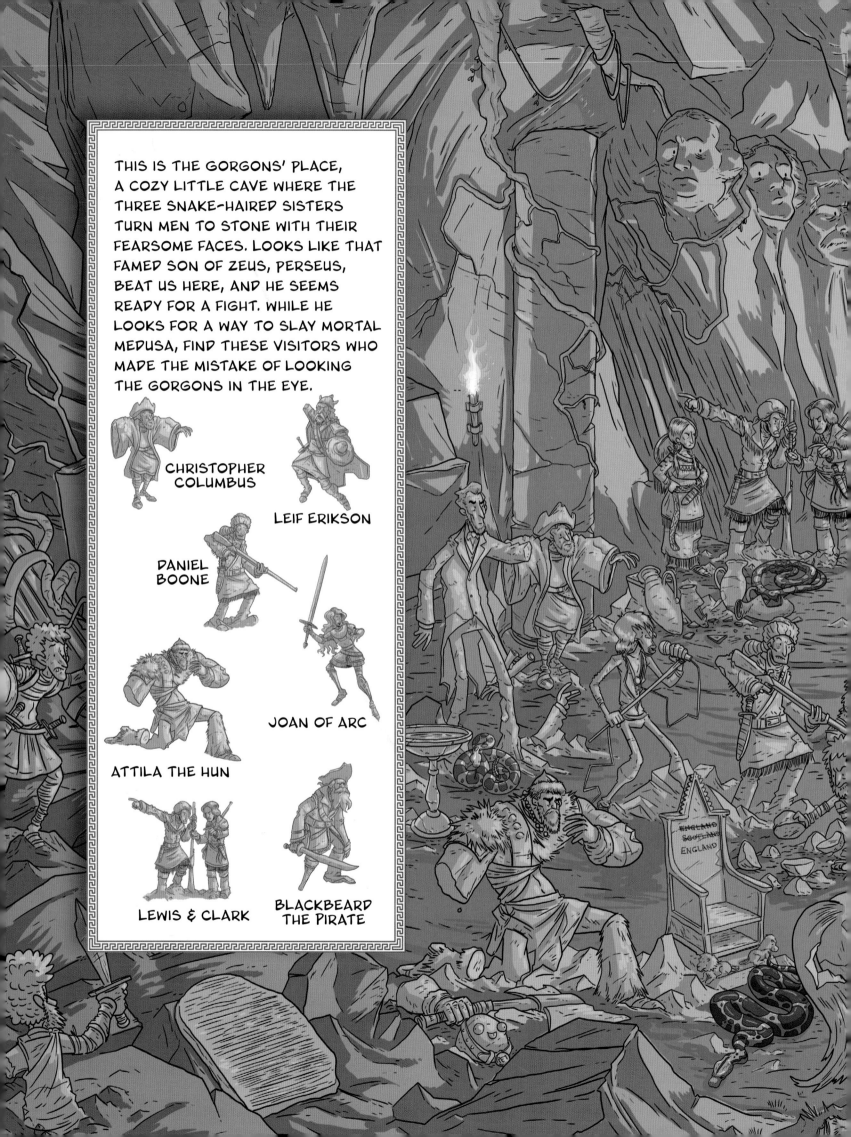

THIS IS THE GORGONS' PLACE, A COZY LITTLE CAVE WHERE THE THREE SNAKE-HAIRED SISTERS TURN MEN TO STONE WITH THEIR FEARSOME FACES. LOOKS LIKE THAT FAMED SON OF ZEUS, PERSEUS, BEAT US HERE, AND HE SEEMS READY FOR A FIGHT. WHILE HE LOOKS FOR A WAY TO SLAY MORTAL MEDUSA, FIND THESE VISITORS WHO MADE THE MISTAKE OF LOOKING THE GORGONS IN THE EYE.

CHRISTOPHER COLUMBUS

LEIF ERIKSON

DANIEL BOONE

JOAN OF ARC

ATTILA THE HUN

LEWIS & CLARK

BLACKBEARD THE PIRATE

NEXT STOP: TROY, AND ITS MOST RECOGNIZABLE LANDMARK, A GIANT WOODEN HORSE GIVEN BY THE GREEKS. TOO BAD THE TROJANS DIDN'T KNOW THAT THOSE WILY GREEK SOLDIERS HID INSIDE AND SNEAKED INTO THE CITY! AS THE TWO SIDES ATTEMPT TO WORK THINGS OUT, LOOK AROUND THE BATTLEFIELD FOR THESE OTHER WOODEN ANIMALS.

ELEPHANT

PIG

DOG

CAT

MOUSE

COW

DUCK

WHO WILL WIN? CASSANDRA KNOWS

AFTER A LONG BATTLE, A HERO JUST WANTS TO GO HOME. UNFORTUNATELY FOR ODYSSEUS HERE, THE GODS WON'T BE MAKING THAT TOO EASY FOR HIM. AT LEAST HE'LL BE TRAVELING IN STYLE! STEP ABOARD HIS SHIP, *THE ODYSSEY*, AND SEARCH FOR SOME OF THE CREATURES WHO WILL MAKE THIS RIDE A JOURNEY TO REMEMBER.

CALYPSO

SIREN

CYCLOPS

CIRCE

POSEIDON

CHARYBDIS

SCYLLA

WHEN A HUMAN, HERO OR VILLAIN ALIKE, REACHES THE END OF HIS JOURNEY, HE COMES TO THE UNDERWORLD, WHERE HADES RUNS THE SHOW. LOOKS LIKE THE FERRYMAN CHARON IS BRINGING IN SOME NEW SHADES. WHILE HADES AND PERSEPHONE WELCOME THE NEW RESIDENTS, SEE IF YOU CAN SPOT THESE SHADES THAT ARE ALREADY HERE.

STABBICUS

DMITRI FELONHISHEADICUS

ALEXANDER THE NOT-SO-GREAT

IRIS IWERNTDEDICUS

JOAQUIN PNEUMONIACUS

ARISTOMPEDONME

DINAH BROKENHARTOLUS

Climb back up Mount Olympus and look for these items the gods and goddesses use to do their jobs.

Aphrodite's love potion

Eros's arrows

Athena's book of wisdom

Hestia's bellows

Apollo's lyre

Hermes's messenger bag

Demeter's grain

Dance on back to the mythological mixer and load your plate with some of these favorite Greek foods.

Dolmades

Baklava

Souvlaki

Greek salad

Olives

Pastitsio

Ambrosia

Keftedes

Heracles trained very hard to be a hero. Parade back to his celebration and look for these things that helped make him so strong.

Spinach

Energy bar

Dumbbells

Coach

Manual

How to Be a Hero

Protein shake

Jump rope

Wind your way back through the labyrinth and look for these fearsome creatures guarding the Minotaur's home.

Echidna

Cyclops

Griffin

Argus

Centaur

Gorgon

Slither back to the home of the serpent-haired Gorgon sisters and search for these snakes.

Anaconda

Viper

Coral snake

Rattlesnake

Python

King cobra

Black mamba

Boa constrictor

Gallop back to the Trojan War and look for these other horses around the battlefield.

Race horse

Horse whisperer

Horse of a different color

Rocking horse

Horse costume

Dark horse

Horse-drawn carriage

Odysseus's crewmates have had an exhausting adventure. Sail back to *The Odyssey* and search for these sailors enjoying the relaxing journey home...while it lasts.

The Underworld is guarded by a ferocious-looking three-headed dog named Cerberus. Descend into Hades's realm once more and look for these things he's provided for the pup.

Collars

Ball

Brush

Bowls

Bones

Leash

Treats

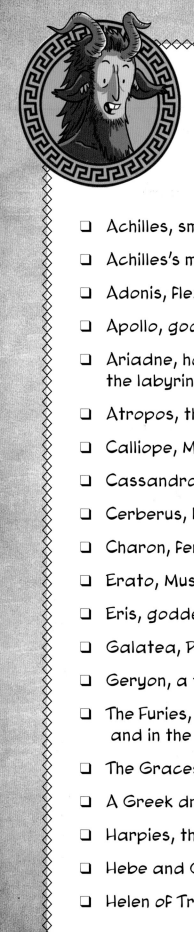

# THINK YOU KNOW YOUR MYTHS?

Go back through the book and look
for these additional characters and
items found in the Greek legends:

- ❑ Achilles, smarting from an arrow to the heel
- ❑ Achilles's mother, dipping her child in the river Styx
- ❑ Adonis, flexing his muscles at the party
- ❑ Apollo, god of music, rockin' out
- ❑ Ariadne, handing Theseus the ball of string that leads him through the labyrinth
- ❑ Atropos, the Fate who cuts the thread of life, brandishing her scissors
- ❑ Calliope, Muse of epic poetry, learning about *The Odyssey*
- ❑ Cassandra, ancient fortune teller whom no one believes
- ❑ Cerberus, Hades's three-headed guard dog
- ❑ Charon, ferryman of the river Styx
- ❑ Erato, Muse of love poems, holding a collection of romantic writings
- ❑ Eris, goddess of discord, watching Paris judge three lovely ladies
- ❑ Galatea, Pygmalion's "statuesque" wife
- ❑ Geryon, a three-headed and three-legged beast
- ❑ The Furies, security guards to the gods, keeping order at the party and in the Underworld
- ❑ The Graces, the gods' favorite performers, putting on a show
- ❑ A Greek drama in progress on the cruise
- ❑ Harpies, those winged beasts that haunt the Underworld
- ❑ Hebe and Ganymede, Mount Olympus's version of waitresses
- ❑ Helen of Troy, feeling a bit carried away by the war